MY FREEDOM TRIP

by Frances Park and Ginger Park
Illustrated by Debra Reid Jenkins

Boyds Mills Press
Honesdale, Pennsylvania

For our mother and her mother
—F.P. and G.P.

To the courageous people of Korea and other nations who have risked their lives
to obtain not only their own freedom but also the freedom of others . . .
they are the true heroes
—D.R.J.

Korean words used in this story:
Apa: Father, Papa
Oma: Mother, Mama
yut: a Korean board game played with sticks

Korean characters in the order they appear in this book:

평화 Peace   사랑 Love   희망 Hope
속삼임들 Whispers   여행 Journey   용기 Bravery
약속 Promise   듣기 Listen   자유 Freedom
기다림 Waiting   위험 Danger   전쟁 War
두려움 Fear   그리움 Longing

Text copyright © 1998 by Frances Park and Ginger Park
Illustrations copyright © 1998 by Debra Reid Jenkins

Boyds Mills Press, Inc.
815 Church Street
Honesdale, Pennsylvania 18431
Printed in China

Library of Congress Cataloging-in-Publication Data
Park, Frances.
My freedom trip / by Frances Park and Ginger Park ; illustrated
by Debra R. Jenkins.—1st ed.
[32]p. : col. ill. ; cm.
Summary: Based on the life of the authors' mother, this is the story of
her escape from North Korea.
ISBN 978-1-56397-468-7 (hc) • ISBN 978-1-59078-826-4 (pb)
1. Korea (North)—Biography—Juvenile literature.
[1. Korea (North)—Biography.] I. Park, Ginger. II. Jenkins, Debra R., ill. III. Title.
951.93 / 92-dc21   1998   AC   CIP
Library of Congress Catalog Card Number 97-77911

First edition
First Boyds Mills Press paperback edition, 2010
Book design by Amy Drinker, Aster Designs
The text of this book is set in 15-point Tiepolo.
The illustrations are done in oils on canvas.

20 19 18 17 16 15 14 13 12 11 (hc)
10 9 8 7 6 5 4 3 2 1 (pb)

*Many years ago, when I was a little schoolgirl
in Korea, soldiers invaded my country. The soldiers
drew a big line that divided Korea into two
countries, North Korea and South Korea. In North
Korea we could no longer speak our minds, or
come and go as we pleased. We lost our freedom.
Many of us secretly escaped to South Korea,
the freedom land. This is my story....*

평화

A peaceful sun shone upon my village in North Korea, over rice paddies and pagoda roofs, on pink petals in ponds and quartz stones on the ground.

I walked home from school, down a path where flowering bushes lined the road and a soft breeze carried butterflies.

It was a beautiful day. The sky seemed endless, and my eyes were soaring! From here, the world looked as free as the doves swiftly dipping into treetops.

But one by one my classmates had been missing from school. First Eumi, then Eunook, then Miyook. My best friends! They had left their homes in the middle of the night to cross the border to the freedom land.

Now I walked home alone.

속삭임들

Then one night my father came to my room and gently woke me. It was so dark that I could not see his face. He spoke softly.

"Tonight I must go on a trip. A man named Mr. Han will guide me to South Korea. He knows of a secret passage where I will cross the border at the shallow end of a river."

"*Apa,*" I wailed, "do not go!"

My father stroked my hair. His fingers were trembling. "Soon, very soon, Mr. Han will return for you, Soo. And he will take you on your freedom trip. Then it will be your mother's turn."

"But why can't we go together?" I pleaded.

"Only one of us can go at a time," he tried to explain. "Less people means less danger of being captured by soldiers."

What was *danger*? It sounded as deep and dark and cold as a river.

My father kissed my cheek, then left my side. He stood in the doorway for a long time.

"I will be waiting for you on the other side of the river," he promised.

기다림

My mother and I awaited word of my father. Every morning we sipped barley tea, wondering where he was. Every evening we played *yut*, still wondering.

One evening full of moon and warm winds, we heard a *tap, tap, tap*.

My mother dropped her *yut* sticks and rushed to open the door.

두려움

A man in white peasant clothing stood in the doorway. On his back he carried a big heavy sack. Behind him the sky was haunting.

As the man stepped inside, I stepped back. He towered over me. Then his face broke into a gentle smile.

"Do not be afraid, Soo," he spoke. "I am Mr. Han, your guide. I bring news of your father."

My mother held her heart.

"Your father is safely settled in the freedom land," he told me. "He is waiting for you."

사랑

My mother quietly rejoiced, then began packing my knapsack with jelly candy, fruit, and clothing.

"Tonight you go on your freedom trip, Soo," she carefully announced. "Now quickly, you must change your clothes."

"*Oma*," I begged, "come with me!"

She cupped my face and whispered, "Do not worry." Her breath was as warm and soothing as tea. "Mr. Han will return for me, and we will be reunited."

My mother hugged me. I could feel her heart beating against mine like a dying dove.

"Be brave, Soo!" she cried.

My freedom trip began by train.

Mr. Han took my hand. Silently, we boarded.
The train was crowded with passengers bumping
into one another. No one spoke or let their
eyes meet.

I looked out the window. Farms and villages
seemed to speed by me. Already I missed my
mother's touch. Already our parting seemed like
a lifetime ago!

The train came to a stop at the foot of a
tall, rocky mountain. Mr. Han secretly nodded.
Then we slipped away from the train and into
the night.

Up the mountain we walked, with the cries
of wild animals in our ears and the moon in our
eyes. The woods were all around us.

Every few moments, Mr. Han would stop and
listen for footsteps. I would listen, too.

We were as still as rocks.

Then he would wink at me and we would
continue up the mountain.

All at once footsteps were upon us!

Mr. Han and I crouched in bushes, not breathing. We watched the long shadows of soldiers creep along a row of rocks.

Were we in danger?

When the shadows disappeared and the footsteps grew distant, Mr. Han whispered, "The soldiers can spot our shadows on the ground because the moon is bright tonight." Sorrowfully, he squeezed my hand. "We must hide here, Soo, until the moon has fallen from the sky."

그리움

Mr. Han opened his sack. Then he put a blanket around me and began peeling fruit in the moonlight.

How I longed for my father! How I wished he could come and carry me across the river to the freedom land. How I longed for my mother! How I wished I was back home playing *yut* with her.

In a gust of wind, her last words came to me—*Be brave, Soo*!

In time the moon vanished behind the mountain.

All was dark over Korea. Mr. Han took my hand. We were like owls, looking everywhere.

We walked until daylight touched the mountainside with grass and wildflowers and four-leafed clovers, until the sound of rushing water reached my ears.

"I can hear the river," I whispered.

Mr. Han nodded knowingly. "You are close to freedom, Soo."

Suddenly, leaves rustled.

We stopped and listened for footsteps. Mr. Han's hand trembled in mine.

Were we in danger?

A soldier leaped into our path! His eyes darkened as he raised his weapon.

"Halt!" he demanded. "Turn around and go back to your village!"

Mr. Han pleaded with him. "I will go back. But please let the child go. Her father is waiting for her across the river."

"No one is allowed to cross the river!" the soldier shouted.

"I beg you, let the child go," Mr. Han continued to plead. "She has come a long way without sleep."

The soldier's attention turned to me. I did not move. I did not speak. The mountain was so quiet I could hear a breeze pass through the trees. It carried my mother's message—
Be brave, Soo!

After a long, silent spell, the soldier lowered his weapon. He looked away from me. I heard him whisper, "Go quickly, child."

Mr. Han guided me toward a dark, mossy opening in the woods. "I must go back, but you are free, Soo. Go! Go!"

I ran without thinking. I was so frightened I forgot where I was going.

Then I saw the river. The water was so blue, my eyes were swimming in every direction! And there was my father, waving wildly from the other side. The freedom land!

"Soo! Soo!" he cried out.

"*Apa*!" I cried back.

I rushed into the river, embracing the sun and the sky.

I was free!

전쟁

Shortly after my freedom trip, soldiers were posted all along the border, and my mother was forced to stay in North Korea.

Soon the Korean War broke out. The war was bigger than any mountain and more haunting than any sky. When the fighting ended, my country was still divided.

I never saw my mother again. How could we have known that the river I crossed would separate us forever?

Many years have passed. I am no longer a little schoolgirl.

But I still think about Mr. Han, my gentle guide,

and about the soldier who set me free.

Mostly, I think about my mother.

When the evening is full of moon and warm winds,

I can still hear her cry—Be brave, Soo!

Brave for the rest of my life.